A NOTE TO PARENTS

When your children are ready to "step into reading," giving them the right books—and lots of them—is as crucial as giving them the right food to eat. **Step into Reading Books** present exciting stories and information reinforced with lively, colorful illustrations that make learning to read fun, satisfying, and worthwhile. They are priced so that acquiring an entire library of them is affordable. And they are beginning readers with an important difference—they're written on four levels.

Step 1 Books, with their very large type and extremely simple vocabulary, have been created for the very youngest readers. **Step 2 Books** are both longer and slightly more difficult. **Step 3 Books,** written to mid-second-grade reading levels, are for the child who has acquired even greater reading skills. **Step 4 Books** offer exciting nonfiction for the increasingly proficient reader.

To Lucy,
who is
full of surprises

Library of Congress Cataloging-in-Publication Data: Prager, Annabelle. The surprise party. (Step into reading. A Step 2 book) SUMMARY: A little boy tries to plan his own surprise birthday party. [1. Birthdays—Fiction. 2. Parties—Fiction] I. De Paola, Tomie, ill. II. Title. III. Series: Step into reading. Step 2 book. PZ7P8864Su 1988 [E] 87-20649 ISBN: 0-394-89596-7 (pbk.); 0-394-99596-1 (lib. bdg.)

Manufactured in the United States of America
    4 5 6 7 8 9 0

STEP INTO READING is a trademark of Random House, Inc.

Step into Reading

THE SURPRISE PARTY

By Annabelle Prager

Illustrated by Tomie de Paola

A Step 2 Book

Random House 🏠 New York

CHAPTER ONE

"Know what?" said Nicky.

"No, what?" said Albert.

"My birthday is coming,"
Nicky told Albert.

"I am going to have
a birthday party."

"Great!" said Albert.

"Are you going to invite me?"

"Of course I am going to invite you,"
said Nicky.

He took out his list.

"I'm going to invite you and Ann,

and Jenny and Jan,

and Morris and Doris,

and Dan."

"That sure is a lot of people,"

said Albert.

"You have to have a lot of people

at a birthday party,"

said Nicky.

"That way you get a lot of presents.

Come on. I need you to help me."

Albert and Nicky

went to Nicky's house.

Nicky took out his bank.

He shook it upside down.

Out fell a quarter and two dimes.

"Oh, no," he said.

"This is not enough money

for a party."

"What are you going to do?"

said Albert.

"I'll think of something,"

said Nicky.

Suddenly his face broke into a smile.

"I know," he said.

"I'll have a surprise party."

"A surprise party for who?"

asked Albert.

"A surprise party for me," said Nicky.

The next day Albert and Nicky

met at the playground.

"I've been thinking," said Albert.

"You can't give a surprise party

for yourself.

You won't be surprised."

"Of course I can't give

a surprise party for myself,"

said Nicky. "But YOU can.

You and Ann, and Jenny and Jan,

and Morris and Doris, and Dan."

"How are we going to do that?"

asked Albert.

Nicky started swinging on a swing.

"Easy," said Nicky. "You say—

Listen, you guys.

Nicky's birthday is coming.

Let's give him a surprise party.

"Then they'll say—

What a good idea.

We love surprise parties.

Albert can bring the cake.

Ann can bring the ice cream.

Jenny can bring the..."

"Oh, I get it," said Albert.

"Everyone will bring something.

What a good idea."

Nicky and Albert
started out of the playground.
"You can get the party ready
at my house.
I will be out
having my tuba lesson,"
Nicky said.
"When I come home you will yell
SURPRISE!
Know what, Albert?
I'll be very surprised
if this doesn't turn out to be
the best surprise party
that ever was."

CHAPTER TWO

Albert ran home to call up Ann,

and Jenny and Jan,

and Morris and Doris,

and Dan.

Sure enough, they all said,

"What a good idea!

We love surprise parties."

They all met at Albert's house
to plan the party.

"We can fix the party
at Nicky's house,"
Albert said.
"He will be out
having his tuba lesson.
When he comes home
we will yell SURPRISE!"
Just then the telephone rang.
Albert answered it.
"Hello," he said.

It was Nicky.

"I forgot to tell you something,"
said Nicky.

"I love balloons
with HAPPY BIRTHDAY on them."

"Okay," said Albert nervously.

"Good-bye."

"Who was that?" asked Ann.

Albert thought very fast.

"Uh…that was my Aunt Belinda,"

he said.

"Shall we have balloons

with HAPPY BIRTHDAY on them?"

"Yes, yes, yes!" shouted everyone.

Ting-a-ling-a-ling.

The phone rang again.

Albert answered it again.

It was Nicky again.

"Can we have snappers?"

asked Nicky.

"The kind that go bang

when you pull them?"

"Sure, Aunt Belinda," said Albert.

Albert slammed down the phone.

He turned to the group.

"Shall we have snappers?" he asked.

"Do you mean the kind that go bang

when you pull them?" said Jenny.

"They're so scary. I love them."

Ting-a-ling-a-ling.

"Let me answer it," said Jan.

"No, no, no!" cried Albert.

He grabbed the phone.

It was Nicky again.

"Be sure that everyone

brings a present," said Nicky.

"And remember

my favorite color is blue."

"Of course, Aunt Belinda,"

said Albert.

"GOOD-BYE!"

"Why does your aunt call you
every five minutes?"
asked Morris and Doris.
"My Aunt Belinda is very lonely,"
said Albert.

"Now, let me think," said Albert.

"Nicky's favorite color is blue.

I am going to make

a beautiful blue birthday cake."

"Do we have to bring

a present?" asked Dan.

"Of course," said Albert.

"Everyone has to bring a present.

Oh, boy, will Nicky be surprised!"

CHAPTER THREE

The next day

Nicky and Albert

were roller skating in the park.

"It will be awful

if anyone finds out

that I know about the party!"

said Nicky.

"Shush," said Albert.

"Here comes Ann

   on her pogo stick."

   Nicky gave a little smile.

"I'd better make sure

   that Ann doesn't think

   I know about the party,"

   he said.

Ann stopped hopping.

"Hi," she said.

"Hi, Ann," said Nicky.

"Guess what I am doing

on my birthday."

Ann gave Albert a worried look.

"What?" she asked.

"My tuba teacher is taking me

to a concert," said Nicky.

"Oh, NO," said Ann.

"Why do you say Oh, NO?"
asked Nicky.

"Don't you like concerts?"

"What I meant to say," said Ann,

"was, Oh, no—no kidding. Excuse me.
I have to go and see Jenny and Jan,
and Morris and Doris, and Dan."

Ann got on her pogo stick

and hopped away

as fast as she could.

Nicky laughed and laughed.

"I fooled her," he said.

"Now nobody can possibly think

that I know about the party.

Oh, I can't wait

for my birthday to come."

CHAPTER FOUR

Three days later

Nicky was walking home

from his tuba lesson.

It was his birthday.

He gave a little skip of excitement.

The day of the party

had finally come!

When Nicky got

to his little house,

it was all dark.

His heart was going

thump thump thump.

"I'd better act very surprised,"

thought Nicky.

"Or everyone will think

I know about the party."

He practiced making

a surprised face.

Then he opened his front door
very slowly.

Nothing happened.

He went into his living room
very slowly.

Nothing happened.

He turned on the light.

Nobody was there.

"Where's the party?" he wondered.

"Oh, I bet they are hiding."

He waited and waited.

Nothing happened.

All of a sudden

the doorbell rang.

"There they are!"

he thought happily.

He practiced making

more surprised faces

on the way to the door.

It was Albert, all alone.

"Where is my party?"

shouted Nicky.

"Oh, Nicky," said Albert.

"It is awful.

Ann told everyone

that you were going to a concert

with your tuba teacher.

So they called off the party."

"Oh, my," cried Nicky.

"Oh, my beautiful surprise party."

A big tear ran down his cheek.

"Don't feel too bad,"

Albert said.

"They are going to have the party

on your next birthday.

You can look forward to it

for twelve whole months."

"I should never have played a trick

on my friends," cried Nicky.

"Never mind," said Albert.

"I made a cake for you anyway.

Come to my house and we can eat it."

CHAPTER FIVE

They walked to Albert's house.

Albert opened his front door.

Nicky went in.

Albert turned on the light.

"SURPRISE! SURPRISE!"

shouted Ann,

and Jenny and Jan,

and Morris and Doris,

and Dan.

Nicky looked all around him.

There were balloons

with HAPPY BIRTHDAY on them.

There was a table

with a blue paper tablecloth

and blue paper plates.

By each plate

there was a red snapper

and a little basket of candy.

Best of all,

there was a pile of presents.

Each one was tied with a big bow.

And each one had a surprise inside.

"Wow!" said Nicky.

"Know what?"

said Albert.

"No, what?"

said Nicky.

"You said you wanted

   the best surprise party that ever was,"

said Albert.

"So we made it a surprise!"